The First Bear

This book is dedicated to brave bears everywhere
who stay with their children no matter what happens — F. H.

For my daughter Catherine.
Wherever the stars may guide you, I will always love you — A. C.

Barefoot Books
37 West 17th Street
4th Floor East
New York, New York 10011

Text copyright © 2000 by Felicity Hansen
Illustrations copyright © 2000 by Anthony Carnabuci

The moral right of Felicity Hansen to be identified as the author and
Anthony Carnabuci to be identified as the illustrator
of this work has been asserted

This book is printed on 100% acid-free paper
The illustrations were prepared in oil paint

Graphic design by Jennie Hoare, England
Typeset in Garamond Book 14pt
Color separation by Bright Arts Graphics, Singapore
Printed and bound in Singapore by Tien Wah Press (Pte) Ltd

1 3 5 7 9 8 6 4 2

U.S. Cataloging-in-Publication Data (Library of Congress Standards)

Hansen, Felicity.
 The first bear / written by Felicity Hansen ; illustrated by
Anthony Carnabuci. —1st ed.
[32]p. : col. ill. ; cm.
Summary: the story of the first bear, who is sent to earth to keep a
lonely child company, and who never wants to leave.
ISBN 1-84148-012--6
1. Bears -- Fiction. I. Carnabuci, Anthony, ill. II. Title.
[E] --dc21 2000 AC CIP

The First Bear

written by
Felicity Hansen

illustrated by
Anthony Carnabuci

walk
the way of wonder...
Barefoot Books

This is the story of how the first bear came into the world. The Great Bear lived up in the sky. No one could remember a time when he had not been there. At night, when the sun had gone to bed, he shone down on the earth, for the Great Bear is all made of stars and he shines brightly in the darkness.

Because he was so high up, the Great Bear could see everything that was happening on the earth. But he did not always like what he saw. While some children lay peacefully in their beds, others lay awake. The Great Bear knew that these children were sad and lonely, because he could see them crying.

"I wish there was something I could do," thought the Great Bear. But he could not go down and comfort the children because he is made of stars, and stars cannot leave the sky.

One night, the Great Bear was watching
over a boy who had no father or mother
and lived with his aunt. The aunt knew
it was her duty to look after the boy, but
she did not really want to. The boy was
crying and crying because he was so
unhappy.

"I wonder how I can comfort this poor
child," thought the Great Bear. "I wonder
if I could send him someone to stop
him from feeling so lonely?"

The Great Bear looked around and saw a small cloud, colored gold by the setting sun. The Great Bear sucked in his breath, and the little cloud floated toward him. He sucked in his breath again, and the cloud came close enough to reach. He took it gently in his starry paws and made it into the shape of a bear. It was a soft, golden color, with warm, brown eyes.

The Great Bear held the first bear close against the star that was his heart. The bear sneezed and blinked. "Bless you!" said the Great Bear as the first bear took his first breath.

Then the Great Bear told the first bear why he had made him.

"I am going to send you to earth to be a friend to a lonely boy," said the Great Bear. "I may be far away, but I shall watch over you both and make sure you do not come to any harm. You must take good care of the boy, but remember: as soon as he leaves home, you must come back to me. Otherwise, something bad might happen. You might get locked up in a dusty attic with the rest of his toys, or even thrown away. So, as soon as the boy packs all his things in a suitcase, you must go outside that very night. I'll see you and bring you back up here, and you will become a new star."

Then the Great Bear called to the Moon, and the Moon shone a moonbeam down through the boy's bedroom window. The Great Bear put the first bear at the top of the moonbeam and the first bear slid — wheeee! — all the way down and landed — bump! — on the boy's bed.

The boy was very surprised and stopped crying. The first bear bowed rather shakily.

"Hello," he said. "I'm your bear."

And the boy laughed.

The first bear and the boy lived together for a long time. The Great Bear was very pleased with his idea, because now the boy never cried at night. Instead, he cuddled his bear, who told him wonderful stories. Together, they planned all kinds of adventures for the next day. Sometimes at night, when the boy was asleep, the first bear would creep out into the yard and tell the Great Bear about all of their adventures.

Then one night, the boy cried again. There was a suitcase in the middle of the room and a large trunk with his name painted on it. The boy was being sent away to boarding school. He would only come home for vacations, he told the first bear. Then the first bear cried too. He knew that he ought to leave the boy and go back to the Great Bear. He thought about becoming a new star and how lovely that would be, but he knew he could not leave his boy to go off to a strange place all by himself.

Quickly — very quickly, so as not to change his mind — the first bear jumped into the trunk and burrowed his way right down to the bottom. He put his paws over his eyes to make sure that the Great Bear could not see him.

The boy found a safe place for his bear at school. Every night, he would climb into the boy's bed and tell him stories, but he never went out to tell the Great Bear what they had been doing.

Far away in the night sky, the Great Bear worried about the first bear. He looked all around the boy's house but he could not see the first bear anywhere, even in the attic. When the aunt took out the garbage, he looked to see if there was a golden ear or paw peeking out anywhere. He asked the Moon, but she had not seen the first bear either.

The Great Bear was so lonely without the first bear that he searched for him night after night. At last, he found the school where the first bear and the boy were staying. The Great Bear called down softly from the sky, "First bear, first bear, are you all right? Please come outside and talk to me. I'm not cross with you. I miss you."

The first bear heard him and crept outside. He, too, had missed his talks with the Great Bear.

"I'm sorry," the first bear said right away. "I didn't do what you said. The boy had to come to this school and I knew he'd be lonely again without me. You sent me to be his friend, and friends share everything. I want to stay with him always. We're both happy now."

The Great Bear listened carefully. At last, he said, "I don't know what to do. You see, everything was going so well that I have made thousands of little bears. I want every child to have one. But how can I be sure that the bears will be all right? If the boy's aunt had found you after he had left, she would have thrown you away. That was why I asked you to come back to me."

"But if the aunt had had a bear of her own when she was little, perhaps she would have been kinder," said the first bear. "If you don't send out the other bears you have made, won't more children grow up just like her? I think you should send them anyway."

Then the first bear stopped. After all, he was just a little bear, telling the Great Bear what to do. But the Great Bear did not seem to mind. "All right," he said, "I'll send out all the little bears so that every child can have one. If your boy can keep you safe, maybe the other children can do the same for their bears."

And so it happened. Soon, thousands of lonely children had bears for company, and they all took good care of them.

As for the boy and the first bear, they stayed together always. When the boy grew up and had children of his own, he searched and searched until he found just the right bear for each baby, and tucked it into the crib. He did the same for his grandchildren, and he would have done the same for his great grandchildren. But by then the boy had become an old, old man and soon it would be time for him to leave the earth.

One very dark night, the first bear took his old friend out into the yard. The Great Bear lifted them both up into the sky and made them into new stars. And to this day, bears on earth look up at the sky on clear nights so that they can see, cradled in the constellation of the Great Bear, the stars that are the first bear and his child.